leapfrog

The Frog Prince

Retold by Hilary Robinson

W
FRANKLIN WATTS
LONDON•SYDNEY

This book is due for return on or before the last date shown below.

First published in 2005 by
Franklin Watts
96 Leonard Street
London
EC2A 4XD

Franklin Watts Australia
Level 17/207 Kent Street
Sydney
NSW 2000

Text © Hilary Robinson 2005
Illustration © Jane Abbott 2005

A CIP catalogue record for this book is available
from the British Library.

ISBN 0 7496 6156 9 (hbk)
ISBN 0 7496 6168 2 (pbk)

Series Editor: Jackie Hamley
Series Advisor: Dr Barrie Wade
Series Designer: Peter Scoulding

Printed in China

For Ginni, who likes woods and wells – H.R.

To Molly and Zachary, my budding
little artists – J.A. (Mummy)

Long ago, in a castle
by a wood, lived a
beautiful Princess.

Deep in the wood was
a wishing well.

The Princess liked to play
with her golden ball there.

One day, she threw her
golden ball too high ...

... and it fell into the well.

The Princess cried and cried. Then she heard a little voice.

"Don't cry," croaked a frog.
"I will find your ball if you
promise to be my friend."

"I promise to be your
friend always if you find
my ball!" said the Princess.

The frog jumped into the well and found the Princess's golden ball.

But when he gave it to the Princess, she ran back to the castle.

The next day, there was a knock at the castle door.

"Princess, Princess, please let me in," croaked a voice.

When the Princess saw the
frog, she slammed the door.

"Who was that?"
asked the King.
"An ugly frog," replied
the Princess.

"I promised I'd always be his friend if he found my golden ball for me."

"Well, if he found your ball, then you must keep your promise," said the King.

So the frog came in and
sat beside the Princess.

At dinner, the frog ate
from the Princess's plate.

That night, he jumped onto
her bed to sleep beside her.

"Go away!" she cried.
But as she pushed the frog
away, he turned into a ...

... handsome Prince!
The Prince told her that a
witch had turned him into
a frog and made him live
in the well.

Only the touch of a
Princess's hand could
break the spell.

The Prince and Princess
soon fell in love.

And they lived happily
ever after.

Leapfrog has been specially designed to fit the requirements of the National Literacy Strategy. It offers real books for beginning readers by top authors and illustrators.
There are 37 Leapfrog stories to choose from:

The Bossy Cockerel
ISBN 0 7496 3828 1

Bill's Baggy Trousers
ISBN 0 7496 3829 X

Mr Spotty's Potty
ISBN 0 7496 3831 1

Little Joe's Big Race
ISBN 0 7496 3832 X

The Little Star
ISBN 0 7496 3833 8

The Cheeky Monkey
ISBN 0 7496 3830 3

Selfish Sophie
ISBN 0 7496 4385 4

Recycled!
ISBN 0 7496 4388 9

Felix on the Move
ISBN 0 7496 4387 0

Pippa and Poppa
ISBN 0 7496 4386 2

Jack's Party
ISBN 0 7496 4389 7

The Best Snowman
ISBN 0 7496 4390 0

Eight Enormous Elephants
ISBN 0 7496 4634 9

Mary and the Fairy
ISBN 0 7496 4633 0

The Crying Princess
ISBN 0 7496 4632 2

Jasper and Jess
ISBN 0 7496 4081 2

The Lazy Scarecrow
ISBN 0 7496 4082 0

The Naughty Puppy
ISBN 0 7496 4383 8

Freddie's Fears
ISBN 0 7496 4382 X

Cinderella
ISBN 0 7496 4228 9

The Three Little Pigs
ISBN 0 7496 4227 0

Jack and the Beanstalk
ISBN 0 7496 4229 7

The Three Billy Goats Gruff
ISBN 0 7496 4226 2

Goldilocks and the Three Bears
ISBN 0 7496 4225 4

Little Red Riding Hood
ISBN 0 7496 4224 6

Rapunzel
ISBN 0 7496 6147 X*
ISBN 0 7496 6159 3

Snow White
ISBN 0 7496 6149 6*
ISBN 0 7496 6161 5

The Emperor's New Clothes
ISBN 0 7496 6151 8*
ISBN 0 7496 6163 1

The Pied Piper of Hamelin
ISBN 0 7496 6152 6*
ISBN 0 7496 6164 X

Hansel and Gretel
ISBN 0 7496 6150 X*
ISBN 0 7496 6162 3

The Sleeping Beauty
ISBN 0 7496 6148 8*
ISBN 0 7496 6160 7

Rumpelstiltskin
ISBN 0 7496 6153 4*
ISBN 0 7496 6165 8

The Ugly Duckling
ISBN 0 7496 6154 2*
ISBN 0 7496 6166 6

Puss in Boots
ISBN 0 7496 6155 0*
ISBN 0 7496 6167 4

The Frog Prince
ISBN 0 7496 6156 9*
ISBN 0 7496 6168 2

The Princess and the Pea
ISBN 0 7496 6157 7*
ISBN 0 7496 6169 0

Dick Whittington
ISBN 0 7496 6158 5*
ISBN 0 7496 6170 4

* hardback